I CAN DO HARD THINGS TOO

WRITTEN BY
ULYSSES GRANT

DEDICATION

This book is dedicated to all the children who have fallen and gotten back up to continue their journey in life, and to all the adults who have fallen and gotten back up to continue their journey in life, and **to the adults who have help those children and other adults** who have fallen and gotten back up, to continue their journey in life.

A Special Heartfelt Thanks To:

My best friend, soulmate and my wife Liz who has supported me when I was down and always helped me back up to say to myself that "I Can Do Hard Things Too!"

Author Copyrights and Credits

Written by
Ulysses **(Horace)** Grant

I CAN
DO HARD
THINGS
TOO

The world's a wild
and crazy place
with much to learn
and do.
But please believe
you can succeed.
Say, "I Can Do
Hard Things Too."

Of course, at times, you'll feel afraid when trying something new. But if in doubt, just shout aloud, "Hey, I Can Do Hard Things Too."

If someone says,
"You're way too small,"
it's just their
point of view.
Say, "Height is not
important, friend,
cos I Can Do
Hard Things Too."

At school, you'll study long and hard, as everyone must do. So, when you feel the pressure's on, think, "I Can Do Hard Things Too."

You're just as smart
as anyone.
It doesn't matter who.
So, listen to the
voice inside say,
"I Can Do
Hard Things Too."

But do I have the strength, you'll ask, to keep on pushing through. What's that you hear inside your ears? "Hey, I Can Do Hard Things Too."

And when the workload
weighs you down
and leaves you
feeling blue.
Just tell yourself,
"I've got this
and I Can Do
Hard Things Too."

For sure, you'll take
some tumbles,
maybe more than
just a few.
Just get up, and
say to yourself,
"I Can Do
Hard Things Too."

As life is like
a rocky road.
not every step is true.
But trust the words
that you have heard
"Yes, I Can Do
Hard Things Too."

So, carry on full speed ahead with God's strength inside of you. And with his guidance and your faith who knows what you can do?

I CAN DO HARD THINGS TOO

ABOUT THE AUTHOR:

Ulysses (Horace) Grant is a native Texan. Ulysses is a graduate of Texas A&M University. After receiving his degree in Journalism and Business Administration and later an MBA, he worked in several industries including Commercial Insurance, Aerospace, Education and more recently Community Services and Head Start. He has several Microsoft and VMware Certifications. Running has always been a passion and as member of the Masters Track & Field Hall of Fame; he still holds World and American Masters Track and Field Records.

Moreover, he describes himself as "always a child at heart" and this has inspired him to write children's books.

Printed in Great Britain
by Amazon

23201430R00016